W9-CKL-827

DATE DUE

THE TWELVE DANCING PRINCESSES

As told by **Marianna Mayer**

Illustrated by **K.Y. Craft**

Morrow Junior Books / New York

Printed in Hong Kong by South China
Printing Company (1988) Ltd.
10
Library of Congress Cataloging-in-Publication Data
Mayer, Marianna.
The twelve dancing princesses.
Summary: When the king's twelve daughters,
under an evil spell, wear holes in their
dancing slippers every night and grow pale and
mysterious, Peter the gardener's boy discovers
their secret and breaks the spell.
[1. Fairy tales.   2. Folklore]   I. Craft,
Kinuko, ill.   II.   Title   III.   Title: 12
dancing princesses.
PZ8.M4514Tw   1989   398.2'2   [E] 83-1034
ISBN 0-688-08051-0
ISBN 0-688-02026-7 (lib. bdg.)
ISBN 0-688-14392-X (pbk.)

To Hope Chatfield

ong ago and far away, at the edge of a humble village, there lived a young farmer named Peter. He was a fine-looking lad; his hair was bleached golden by the sun, and his eyes were the color of the bluest sky. Although he was a skillful farmer, Peter yearned for a life unlike his own. He often dreamed of splendid castles and of doing noble deeds that might win him the love of a fair princess. This made him different from the rest of the villagers; they laughed at him and jokingly called him the Dreamer. But their laughter only increased Peter's desire to leave the village and seek his fortune, whatever it might be.

ne warm day in the middle of summer, as he sat listening to the soft contented braying of his sheep, Peter had a vision: A lovely woman dressed like a queen was standing before him. She spoke gently, calling him by name, "Peter, you must go to the King's castle. If you succeed where others have failed, you shall get your wish and marry a princess."

Peter awoke with a start, but he did not forget his dream. All day he could think of nothing but the regal woman's words. That night, he packed his few belongings and gave his flock of sheep to a kind neighbor. At daybreak, he set out for the King's castle.

Like everyone else, Peter knew the King had twelve daughters, each different from the others and all quite beautiful. Each Princess had many suitors who asked for her hand in marriage, but the twelve sisters always refused every one.

ince they had been very young, all the sisters slept in a large hall, their beds standing one beside the other. At night, when they lay safely tucked in their beds, the King locked their door himself and bolted it securely. It was said that he alone kept the key to their room on a gold chain around his neck.

Yet each day for the past year, when he unlocked their door and kissed them all good morning, he found to his dismay that their satin dancing slippers had been worn to pieces. The King became concerned and asked his daughters, "How can it be that you wear out your brand-new slippers every night?" But his daughters shook their pretty heads and refused to answer.

The King pleaded with his daughters for a reason, but to no avail. He tried scolding and threatening them, but this, too, did no good. He sought clever spies to watch them, but the Princesses kept to themselves and guarded their secret.

Soon the twelve sisters' radiant complexions took on a pale, unearthly light. Where once they had been open and warmhearted, now they grew cold and haughty. An air of mystery filled the castle, and people began to say, "The Princesses are no doubt bewitched." And everyone wondered who might come forward to break the spell.

The King knew of the gossip, and this talk of enchantment angered him, for he was reminded of a half-forgotten prophecy long ago. Exactly a dozen years before, as the Queen lay dying, she called upon a fortune-teller to learn what the future held for her royal daughters.

The wizened old fortune-teller's eyes burned bright, and her thin voice crooned like a haunting echo as she said, *"One through twelve, like the hours on a clock, first to last, twelve daughters you have. All as beautiful as the many months of the year. They are the future!"* The old woman paused to draw a circle upon the floor and then began to toss her divining stones. *"But the twilight will claim them. No mortal love will they know. No earthly happiness will they share. Their secret is hidden between this world and the next. It will not be easily found."*

This prophecy tormented the ailing Queen. To comfort her, the King began to bolt his daughters' bedroom door at night in the hope of shutting out danger. But the mystery of the tattered dancing shoes proved to him that he could not protect his daughters.

inally, the worried King sent out his heralds to proclaim that whoever discovered how the Princesses wore out their shoes could then choose one of them for his wife. Dozens of princes came to the kingdom to take up the challenge. Each in turn was brought by nightfall to a room adjoining the Princesses' bedchamber and left to see what happened to the twelve sisters. By the next morning, the Princesses' slippers were always full of holes, but there was no trace of the prince who had spent the night watching. Each one had vanished, and no one could say where he had gone.

When Peter arrived at the castle, he felt he had no right to offer himself, a common farmer, to the King. Instead, he asked the royal gardener for work within the castle grounds. The gardener thought that such a fine-looking boy might please the King's daughters.

our task will be to tend the Princesses' special flower garden," he said. "And every morning, you must make bouquets to present to each of them."

Peter was delighted with the work. Wherever Peter's gentle hands touched the earth it grew fruitful for him. Flowering vines climbed the castle walls and framed the Princesses' upper windows in thick bowers. And the velvet-petaled violet, the rose, the honey-cupped tulip, and the poppy grew in rioting glory in their garden.

At sunrise, he carefully selected blossoms and placed them in twelve identical baskets. When the Princesses awoke late in the morning, he gave a basket to each, and all but one took the bouquets without even a glance. The youngest, Princess Elise, thanked him graciously. She fixed her amber eyes on him and smiled as she said, "Oh, sisters, look how handsome our new gardener is!"

The others burst out laughing and the eldest sister scolded Elise, "You foolish child! How can you, a Princess, take notice of a common gardener?"

lise's gentle beauty struck Peter. She was small and spirited, her rich black hair fell about her delicate shoulders, and a smile came easily to her lips. From their first meeting, Peter longed to discover the Princesses' secret. Though he heard that those who tried had mysteriously disappeared, the image of Elise made him brave and tempted him to risk his fate.

But how, he wondered, shall I succeed?

Night after night Peter lay awake trying to think of a plan, but to no avail. Many weeks passed, and finally he began to lose faith altogether when one night the same lovely woman appeared before him. "Seek help from what you know best," she said. "Through your own gifts you shall succeed."

When Peter awoke, his dream made little sense to him. Then one day, while working in the royal garden, Peter found a small silver-green plant struggling to grow among the weeds he was clearing. Yet rather than discard it along with the weeds, he nurtured it.

ay after day the fragile plant flourished,   and soon a tiny bud appeared.   When the bud bloomed,   its delicate petals were golden.   Peter thought to give the flower to Elise,   but that afternoon she stayed close to her sisters,   and he had no chance to catch her alone. Disappointed,   Peter took the flower to his own room,   and standing before a mirror,   he placed it in his buttonhole.   Suddenly his image faded and he was invisible.

That night,   Peter used the tiny golden flower to tiptoe unseen behind the twelve Princesses as they went to their bedchamber.   The room was candlelit and spacious.   A fire burned brightly in the huge fireplace,   and twelve canopied beds draped with heavy satin damask stood all in a row.   Quietly Peter crept under a bed to wait.   Soon everything was silent,   save for the ticking of a clock.   Hours passed as the clock struck ten,   eleven,   then twelve.   All of a sudden,   there were the sounds of rustling silk and the sisters' soft laughter.

The eldest said,   "Hurry,   we mustn't be late!"

eter could hear boxes being opened, closets being shut, and the scurrying of slippered footsteps. Finally, the eldest whispered, "Now, are we all ready?"

"Oh, yes," the rest answered.

His heart pounding, Peter peeked out to steal a glance. As he watched, the eldest sister went to her bed and tapped it three times. Magically, it sank beneath the floor, revealing a stairway. Then, beautifully gowned, the twelve Princesses took up the bouquets Peter had made them that morning, and single file, they hurriedly descended the long, winding staircase.

Peter rushed from his hiding place and followed. In his haste he stepped on the hem of Elise's gown.

"Please wait, there is someone behind me," cried Elise. "He has hold of my gown."

"You silly baby, you are afraid of your own shadow tonight," said the eldest, looking back at her. "There is no one there. You have simply caught the hem of your gown with your heel."

hough she was unable to explain her uneasiness, Elise kept looking behind her nervously. But despite her fears, like her sisters she could not resist going on.

The Princesses continued to drift gracefully down the staircase, which took them to the threshold of a world outside their own — a strange and wonderful twilight kingdom. The eldest sister opened a gate covered with vines, and a little silver forest stretched ahead of them.

They quickened their steps as the moon led their way down a narrow footpath. Silently Peter pursued them. Warm, fragrant breezes scented with jasmine filled the air, and under the moonlight pure silver leaves sparkled and danced like musical chimes. Very faintly, Peter heard the sound of violins far in the distance.

Drawing clear of the silver trees, they soon came to a dazzling forest of gold. Thousands of gold leaves caught the light of the moon, and it seemed to be bright golden day instead of silver night. The music was clearer now, and Peter could just catch the sounds of instruments playing a beguiling tune.

Next they crossed to another forest, more stunning than the others, where glittering diamonds clustered upon every leaf. It was as though all the stars in the heavens had come to rest upon these leaves. The music grew stronger still, and all at once the sisters began to run toward the sound.

t last, breathless, they arrived at a large lake. On the shore twelve small boats stood awaiting them, and in each a fine prince was seated. Peter quickly sat himself beside Elise. Grasping the oars, the princes began rowing smoothly across the lake.

Elise's boat went more slowly than the rest since it held an extra passenger. "Why is it that our boat lags behind tonight?" she asked her partner.

"I don't know, but I must row with all my strength and still we are the last," replied the prince.

As they neared the other side of the lake, Peter saw a splendid black marble palace brilliantly lit at every window. The moment the boats touched shore, the music swelled and quickened. Violins, harpsichords, drums, and cymbals joined together to create an irresistible dance melody.

The Princesses took hold of their partners' hands and eagerly skipped into the palace. They entered a huge ballroom where they were greeted by many other young dancers. Gleaming mirrored walls surrounded them and reflected the crystal chandeliers that hung from the high vaulted ceiling.

s the group was swept up by the first dance, Peter felt he had never seen more graceful young men and women. Endlessly they danced on and on, seeming never to tire. Soon even Peter found he was powerless to resist dancing to the hypnotic music. In the shadows, alone and unseen, he followed along in time with the others.

Though Peter admired the loveliness of all the sisters, it was the youngest Princess who seemed to him the most beautiful. Her amber eyes glowed with light as she moved with the music, and it was easy to see that she loved dancing more than anything else in the world. Peter wished that he was her partner and envied the men who danced with her. But he had little cause to be jealous. The sisters' partners were in truth the very princes who had tried to find out their secret. One by one they were each brought to the black marble palace and given a special potion that turned their hearts to ice and left them nothing but a love of dancing.

Just before dawn, the Princesses were forced to stop dancing, for the soles of their new slippers were worn with holes. But a wonderful banquet had been set for them. They ate, laughed, and drank till the eldest sister gathered them together to return home.

Still invisible, Peter took the seat beside Elise, and the princes rowed their boats back across the lake.

**W**hen they arrived, the sisters waved goodbye to their partners, promising to meet again the next night. Then they hurried home following the same path.

But as they were leaving the forest of diamonds, Peter, wishing for proof of all the wonders he had seen that night, broke a small branch from one of the trees. To his horror, a CRACK! like the breaking of glass filled the woods.

"What was that?" cried Elise, whirling around.

"It's nothing but the wind through the trees," said the eldest sister, yawning. "Come, don't keep us waiting for you."

In the forest of gold Peter quietly tried to pull a twig from a golden branch. But a violent SNAP! resounded throughout the woods.

"Stop!" shouted Elise. "Something is very wrong."

But the eldest said, "That is nothing but the distant sound of lightning."

At last they reached the forest of silver. Boldly Peter tore a branch from a silver tree. Suddenly there was the rumbling of thunder all around them.

"Oh, sisters!" cried Elise, standing still. "All night I've felt something strange hovering about us."

ut the eldest answered, "You little mouse, your fears make us all nervous. It's nothing but the clatter of an oncoming storm. Now hurry, we must get home before sunrise."

While she was speaking, Peter was able to slip ahead. He ran up the staircase to the Princesses' room. There he flung open a window and managed to climb down the thick vines that clung to the castle walls. He found himself in the garden below. The sun was rising and already it was time to begin his daily chores.

That day, Peter tucked the branch from the silver tree into Elise's bouquet. When she found it she was startled, though she said nothing to her sisters. Ever since they had first laughed at her for taking notice of Peter, she had avoided him and tried to follow their haughty example. But now when she spied him working in the garden, she went up to him. Then abruptly she changed her mind when she saw her sisters coming, and she hurried away without a word.

he same evening the Princesses again went to the dance and again Peter followed. He crossed in Elise's boat, and this time it was her partner who complained that the boat seemed to fall behind the others.

"It's only the heat that tires you. I feel it myself tonight," Elise said to reassure him.

All through the dance the youngest Princess looked for Peter, but she could not see him. As they came back through the woods, Peter stumbled. This time the eldest sister wondered at the sound.

"It's nothing, sister," replied the youngest calmly.

The very next morning, Elise found a branch from the golden forest in her bouquet. When she saw Peter she stopped to question him, for she had made up her mind that she must deal with him sharply so that these odd events would go no further.

"Tell me, where do the silver and gold branches come from?"

Peter bowed his head and said, "The Princess Elise knows."

"So you have followed us!" The Princess fell silent for a moment, but then continued, "Well, then you know our secret. I must ask you to keep it. But you shall be rewarded by me." With that she hastily brought forth a purse filled with gold and offered it to him.

"Princess, I am your humble servant. I need no reward from you," said Peter quietly. Humiliated, he turned away from her and walked on without touching the gold.

or three whole nights Elise neither saw nor heard anything out of the ordinary. But on the fourth day there was a branch from the diamond forest in her bouquet. Immediately she went to Peter.

"You know what the King has promised to pay for our secret, do you not?" she asked him.

"Yes, your Royal Highness, I do," replied Peter.

"Are you going to tell him?"

Peter shook his head. "No, Princess."

"Is it because you are afraid?"

"No, Princess. I am not frightened."

Elise's eyes flashed with anger as she said, "Then, whatever is the reason?"

But Peter could not answer her. Blushing, he hung his head and would not meet her eyes.

Elise's sisters saw her talking with the garden boy and they began to tease her. "Next you'll be helping him pick flowers for our bouquets," said one. "Indeed, there can be no doubt she's falling in love with the garden boy," said another, laughing.

Elise was so embarrassed that when Peter presented her bouquet the next day, she rudely refused it. However, he was always in her thoughts, and this troubled and confused her. Finally, she decided she must tell her sisters everything.

he other Princesses were furious when they were told. They wanted to have Peter thrown into prison. But Elise threatened to go to their father with the truth if any harm came to the boy. That she should defend him astonished the others, but Elise reasoned that they had nothing to fear. "After all, he hasn't betrayed us, has he?"

They could not deny it, so the twelve sisters devised a plan they could all agree upon. They would invite Peter to the dance with them, as they had the many princes, and there give him the same potion the others had unwittingly taken. Then they sent for Peter. But he knew only too well what they intended, for his golden flower had helped him once again. Without the Princesses' knowledge, he had overheard their discussion.

Now sad but resigned, he came before them. "I would be honored to attend," was all he replied when the Princesses invited him. He had decided if this was what Elise wished, he would not resist.

hen he returned to his room, he found a handsome velvet suit that the Princesses had left for him to wear to the dance that night. As agreed, he went to the King and asked permission to be brought to the room adjoining the Princesses' hall to take the night watch that evening. Peter looked so impressive in his princely suit of clothes that the King was quite willing. No one guessed who he really was.

That night, the twelve sisters went to their bedchamber and Peter was left to wait. At midnight, the eldest sister gave the signal for them to depart. They walked with Peter in the twilight through the silver, gold, and diamond forests, and this time he crossed in the eldest sister's boat. At the black marble palace, the eldest led him out for the first dance. He then danced with each Princess in turn. Peter danced so well and looked so distinguished that everyone was delighted with him. When the moment came for Peter to dance with the youngest Princess, Elise felt he was the best partner she had ever danced with. But she was shy with him and they found it difficult to look at each other.

At the end of their dance Peter whispered, "You needn't have worried. I would never have forced you to marry a common gardener."

lise started to say something in reply. But just then, the eldest sister came forward to take Peter away with her for the next dance.

When the Princesses' dancing slippers were quite worn through, the music ceased. The Princesses and their companions then sat themselves at the banquet table to enjoy a splendid meal. Elise remained silent while her sisters flattered Peter extravagantly on his dancing and his manners. They offered him countless delicious dishes to taste, but Peter found he had no appetite.

At last, the eldest sister made a sign that the special drink was to be presented to Peter. "The twilight kingdom has no secrets from you now and neither do we," she said solemnly. "Let us all drink a toast to welcome you to our group."

For one brief moment, Peter looked directly at Elise and then lifted the goblet to his lips.

"Stop!" Elise cried out. "Don't drink. It will make you like the rest." She took the goblet from him and cast the contents to the floor. With this one act of love the spell was broken and everyone in the palace instantly was free from enchantment. As though shaken from a trance, the entire group rose up in astonishment. The princes' icy hearts melted and they were themselves once more. Filled with sudden relief, the sisters embraced each other and quickly they all made ready to leave.

he twelve boats were crowded as they crossed the lake; that night no one was left behind. Together everyone passed through the beautiful forests, and when they reached the staircase leading back to their own world, the sounds of crumbling stones could be heard in the distance.

Elise squeezed Peter's hand, saying, "We shall never be able to enter the twilight kingdom again."

"Does that make you sad?" asked Peter.

"No," answered Elise, smiling. "We can always dance. But now we have each other, and I have come to love you more than anything else."

When the Princesses told their father what had happened, he was overjoyed. At once he sent his heralds to announce that the mystery was solved—the spell had been broken. Throughout the kingdom the people rejoiced at the news, and that very day Elise and Peter's wedding was celebrated. The other eleven sisters were in attendance, and after the ceremony, naturally, there was the most magnificent ball. Everyone danced through the night till, tired and happy, they all wore out their best dancing shoes. But this time the King didn't mind in the least, to the great delight of the twelve dancing Princesses.